Elmo's New Puppy

By Catherine Samuel · Illustrated by Maggie Swanson

Featuring Jim Henson's Sesame Street Muppets

A GOLDEN BOOK · NEW YORK
Published by Golden Books Publishing Company, Inc.,
in cooperation with Children's Television Workshop

A portion of the money you pay for this book goes to Children's Television Workshop.
It is put right back into SESAME STREET and other CTW educational projects. Thanks for helping!

One sunny morning Big Bird and Elmo were sitting in front of 123 Sesame Street, watching people passing by.

"What's the matter, Elmo?" asked Big Bird. "Why do you look so gloomy on such a sunny day?"

Elmo sighed. "If only Elmo had a puppy, life would be perfect," he said.

Just then, Elmo's neighbor, Mr. Fuzzle, strolled by.
"Excuse me, Elmo," he said. "My family and I are going
on vacation tomorrow. Would you be able to take
care of our puppy while we're away?"

Elmo jumped up. "YipPeee!"

he cried happily.

The next day the Fuzzles knocked on Elmo's door.
"Here's our Phoebe," said Mr. Fuzzle.
    "And here is a list of instructions," said Mrs. Fuzzle.
"Please take good care of her for us!"

"Bye, Phoebe!" said Suzie Fuzzle, giving the puppy a hug and a kiss. "We'll miss you!"

"Thanks again, Elmo!" said Mr. Fuzzle. And off they went.

"Gee," said Elmo. "Elmo finally has a puppy to take care of!" He watched Phoebe chew up the sofa. "You must be hungry, Phoebe. The first thing Elmo needs to do is feed you!"

"Elmo knows puppies have to eat several times a day," panted Elmo as he poured food into Phoebe's dish. "And Elmo will be sure you have plenty of fresh water to drink."

Elmo quickly found out what hard work it was to take care of a puppy. At night Phoebe missed the Fuzzles.

"Elmo knows you want them to come home soon, Phoebe," Elmo whispered sleepily. "Right now Elmo misses them, too."

Elmo missed the Fuzzles even more when he had to
clean up after Phoebe.

Phoebe wanted to go for a walk several times a day.

"How's it going, Elmo?" Big Bird called to him.
But Elmo was too busy to answer.

Finally Elmo's neighbors returned. "Thanks so much,
Elmo!" said Mr. Fuzzle. "I hope Phoebe was no trouble."
"Oh, no," said Elmo. "No trouble at all."

"I guess you must have changed your mind about a puppy, right Elmo?" Big Bird said later that day.

Elmo sighed. "No, Big Bird. Elmo still wants a puppy more than anything."

The next morning Elmo's doorbell rang. When Elmo opened the door, the first thing he saw was a basket with a big ribbon around it. Inside was a thank-you note from the Fuzzle family. And there was something else, too.

"A PUPPY!"

Elmo yelled.

This time Elmo knew just what to do.
"You must be hungry," said Elmo, gently taking his
favorite teddy bear out of the puppy's mouth.

That night the puppy howled. Elmo put a ticking alarm clock in bed with the puppy.

"This should help you sleep," he whispered gently. The soothing sound of the clock calmed the puppy. He curled up in his basket and soon began to snore softly.

"First thing tomorrow, Elmo will take you to the veterinarian for a checkup," Elmo said.

The next day, the veterinarian checked the puppy's eyes and looked inside his ears and mouth. She listened to his heart with a stethoscope. She felt his *tummy* carefully. Then she gave him two shots to protect him from catching animal diseases.

Elmo and his puppy were very brave.

Elmo taught his puppy how to go to the bathroom outside.

He took him for walks.

He played with him.

And Elmo gave his puppy baths when he needed them.

"Hi, Elmo," Big Bird called when they met in the park a few days later. "How's it going?"

Elmo smiled as he watched his puppy playing with Phoebe. "Great, Big Bird," he said. "Say, do you know anyone who has a kitten that needs a new home? Because now Elmo wants a kitty cat, too!"